John Huston Finley

Ellen her Book

Being a Collection of Rhymes about Ellen Boyden Finley & Some of her

Childhood Friends

John Huston Finley

Ellen her Book
Being a Collection of Rhymes about Ellen Boyden Finley & Some of her Childhood Friends

ISBN/EAN: 9783337271152

Printed in Europe, USA, Canada, Australia, Japan

Cover: Foto ©Andreas Hilbeck / pixelio.de

More available books at **www.hansebooks.com**

This is not an "edition de luxe",
(The "fashionable set" among books),
But a modest edition "for love,"
(Though "money" may buy all above
What in love I have printed for her
Whose poet I am,—nor demur);
But more than two hundred, 'tis sure,
Nor money nor love may procure,
For this is the limit, no more
May be had though an angel implore;
And each book bears a number, q. v.,
Signed and sealed in due order by me,

(SEAL) *Her X Father.*

No.

Heaven lies about us in the infancy of our children.—(*Adapted from Wordsworth.*)

Ellen

ELLEN HER BOOK

BEING A COLLECTION OF RHYMES
ABOUT ELLEN BOYDEN FINLEY &
SOME OF HER CHILDHOOD FRIENDS
BY
HER FATHER

THE CAD-   GALESBVRG
MVS PRESS   ILLINOIS
1897   V.S.A.

PVBLISHED FOR THE AVTHOR BY THE CADMVS
PRESS ❧ PVBLISHERS TO THE CADMVS CLUB ❧❧
FOR SALE ONLY AT "THE CADMVS CORNER"
STROMBERG & TENNEY'S ❧ GALESBVRG ❧ ILL'S

PRINTED BY THE WAGONER-MEHLER COMPANY
GALESBVRG ❧ ILLINOIS

PREFACE

There is no need of preface except to make acknowledgment of the artistic contribution of Miss Marion Crandall to the beauty of this book in her sketches; to express appreciation of the quaint Norse-like lullaby by Mr. Arnold Grieg of Edinburg, to which the words of "The Poor Poet" have been sung by him; to thank the editors of a number of periodicals, especially of *The Century, The Independent, The Interior, The Advance,* and *The Chicago Record,* for permission to reprint verses which appeared first in their columns, and to express indebtedness to Mr. Allen Ayrault Green for several photographs made expressly for this collection.

This Book has been written for Ellen. If others find aught of interest or pleasure in it the author will be gratified. But he has full compensation in the future appreciation of this volume of personal and domestic verse by the Little Critic for whose eyes it has been printed and for whose heart it holds many a prayer.

J. H. F.

December 1, 1897.

The Dedication.

DEAR CHILD:
THESE LINES ARE ALL TOO FEW,
TO MEASURE QUITE MY LOVE FOR YOU;
BUT AS ON MAPS THE INCHES' SCALE IS MEANT
TO HINT THE STRETCH OF SEA AND CONTINENT,—
SO LET WHAT'S WRITTEN HERE, OR POOR OR WORSE,
BE MULTIPLIED TO LEAGUES OF ARDENT VERSE,
THAT SHALL O'ERLEAP THE WIDE HORIZON'S RIM
IN VAIN ATTEMPT TO TELL THE LOVE OF HIM
NO LINES OF LATITUDE OR LONGITUDE CAN BOUND
THO' LONG ENOUGH TO REACH
THE WORLD
AROUND

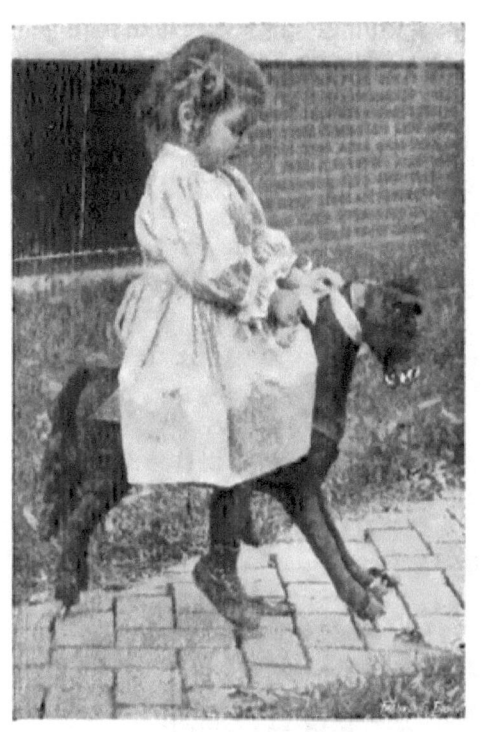

My Pegasus

MY PEGASUS

The Muses keep a livery,
  Hard by the classic fount,
And here's the horse they've let to me
  As my poetic mount.

They call him Pegasus, you know,
  (At home they call him "Peg");
He lost his wings some time ago,
  He's slightly lame of leg.

But he will gallop, trot, or walk,
  (And sometimes even rack);
And never is he known to balk
  With Ellen on his back.

Whene'er we want a Pegasus,
  I'm always satisfied
If they send down a horse to us
  That "any child can ride."

So hear his tiny, pattering feet
  Upon the pavement ring,—
My Pegasus comes down the street,
  My Muse begins to sing.

The Poor Poet

THE
POOR
POET'S
LULLABY

The cupboard's bare, my child; oh, bye,
Bye low;
I hear the wolfie's hungry cry—
Bye low.
So go to sleep, my pretty one,
While father takes his inky gun
And hunts a little bunny-bun
For baby's breakfast.   Bye low, bye,
Bye low!

THE POOR POET'S LULLABY

ARNOLD GRIEG.

There, little one, don't cry; oh, bye,
          Bye low;
Good wood and coal come very high—
          Bye low.
   Your father's got an old "sheepskin"
   To wrap his darling baby in,
   But there's no coal in binny-bin
To cook the bunny-bun.   Oh, bye,
          Bye low !

So father'll write a rhyme, or try,—
          Bye low,—
Which some kind editor will buy,
          Buy low;
   And then he'll take the money-mun
   To catch the little bunny-bun
   And buy a tiny tunny-ton
Of coal to cook it with.   Oh, buy,
          Buy low!

My Blessed Wee Skilligallee

THE LIGHT O' SKILLIGALLEE*

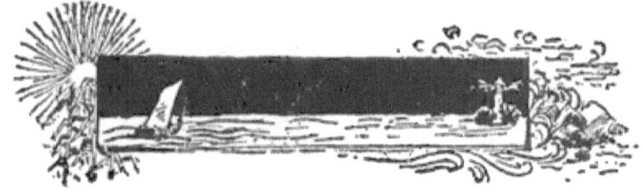

When summer's hot breath wilts the corn
And there's no dewy eve nor morn
To rest a body faint and worn,
I sometimes cross a Northern sea
To bring the spring-time back to me;
    I sail for far Skilligallee,
    The Light o' far Skilligallee,
    That points the way to St. Marie.
        Skilligallig! Skilligallee!

I seek the spring-time with its flowers,
The spring-time with its April showers,
The spring-time with its scented bowers,
The spring that's flown beyond that sea
And carried all away from me,
    Away beyond Skilligallee,
    The Light o' far Skilligallee,
    That points the way to St. Marie.
        Skilligallig! Skilligallee!

---

*A Light-house on the Ile au Galet, far up Lake Michigan, the name of which has been, by the lake sailors, corrupted into "Skilligallig" and "Skilligallee."

Beyond that Light there's rest and peace,
Beyond that Light life takes new lease,
Beyond that Light all troubles cease;
From all that irks, one there is free,
Up there beyond that Northern sea,
    Up there beyond Skilligallee,
    The Light o' far Skilligallee,
    That points the way to St. Marie.
       Skilligallig! Skilligallee!

The years have brought my summer days
With heat and dust, when one oft prays
For spring's cool breath, or autumn's haze;
But God has set a light for me
Just by the side of my life's sea,
    A very small Skilligallee,
    With eyes of my own St. Marie,
    A wee, blue-eyed Skilligallee.
       Skilligallig! Skilligallee!

Though rough the way, though dark the skies,
Whene'er I see those precious eyes,
My courage all the world defies;
I'm young again; from care I'm free;
The spring comes back again to me.
    God keep you long by my life's sea,
    My blessed, wee Skilligallee,
    With eyes of my own St. Marie!
       Skilligallig! Skilligallee!

TO DOMIDUCA*

Oh, thou, who know'st the roads
　That mark the hills and plains,
The place of men's abodes,
　　The highways and the lanes;
　　　The paths that forests thread,
　　　The ways that wild beasts tread,
　　　The stars that shine o'erhead;
　　　The streams in every mood,
　　　The fields by every rood,
　　　The swamps where poisons brood,
　　　　　Wise Domiduca!
Lead home this little one,
　If she should stray,
Keep watch by star and sun,
　Drive harm away,
　　　　Brave Domiduca!
Lead thou, at last, her feet,
　By thy kind light,
To that celestial street
　Where there's no night,
　　　　Dear Domiduca!

---

* One of the "little gods" dear to the Roman home,—she
who watched over one's safe home-coming.

THE FIRST WORD

I've heard the sky-lark singing
  Along his heavenward flight;
I've heard the church-bells ringing
  Upon a Christmas night;
I've heard the mother crooning
  Her dreamy lullaby;
I've heard the saints attuning
  Their praise to Him on high;
I've heard the organ swelling
  With animating sound;
I've heard the fountain welling
  With laughter from the ground;
I've heard the thunders rolling
  Adown Niag'ra's hill;
I've heard the goblins bowling
  Along the Kaaterskill;
I've heard the North-wind moaning
  Among the Norway pines;
I've heard the Fauni droning
  Beneath the Apennines;
I've heard the "angels" thrumming
  On harps of human make;
I've heard old Nature humming
  The tune that cures all ache;
I've heard—but why should I prolong
  This catalogue? For, ah!
There is no other speech nor song
  When Ellen says "Pa-pa."

THE DISCOVERY OF A TOOTH

My father says that Christopher C.
Was the greatest man of his century,
    For he had a notion
    That over the ocean
There was a land—the home of the free—
That wasn't in the geography;
    And so he went and discovered it straight,
    (But found it in a most barbarous state),
    October the twelfth, I think, was the date,
In fourteen ninety-two A. D.—
So my father he says, and he
        Ought to know.

But father says that Christopher C.,
Who guessed at the earth's sphericity,
    Was but such another
    As my little mother,
Who dreamt one day of an island of pearl
Behind the lips of her little girl,
    And so she went and discovered it straight,
    ('Twas set in coral, the records state),
    October the seventh, I think, was the date,
In eighteen ninety-four A. D.—
So my mother she says, and she
        Ought to know.

Eugene Field

We too have a little one in the house — a little girl, and she is just beginning to coo and tell me all about the fairy land she came from. I'm sure one could not have a sweeter treasure than a baby in the house. Sometime I must write some verses for your little one. With every cordial regard, yours sincerely,

Eugene Field.

Chicago, Oct. 30. 1894.

TO EUGENE FIELD

Come, put away thy trumpet, little one,
    And leave thy noisy play,
For he is sleeping, though the autumn sun,
    Has brought another day.

For he is sleeping, thy good friend and mine,
    Who gave this trump of tin
To thee, and that red, noisy drum of thine—
    Thou'lt muffle its harsh din.

For he is sleeping, who with loving pen
    Sat often all night long
To make day brighter for his fellow-men,
    To sweeten life with song.

Thou wouldst not rouse him from his sleep?
    Thou wouldst?
    Ah, child, thou speak'st the ache
My own heart feels. Oh, if with trump thou
    couldst—
    Couldst his long slumber break.

The blare of trumpet and the beat of drum,
    Dear child, he'll hear no more;
His heart's succumbed at last to one who's come
    In silence through his door.

WHERE HOLLYHOCKS GROW

There's a legend very old,
That a precious pan of gold
  Is by fairy hands concealed
Where the rainbow's varied hues
Melt in haze, that all imbues
  With its dyes the distant field.

But no man has found such store,
Though he's digged and hunted o'er
  All the earth to catch its glint;
And I've come to think this meed
Is, forsooth, but rainbow seed,
  Coined in Nature's gen'rous mint.

So where clumps of hollyhock
In their bright-dyed blossoms mock
  Heaven's colors manifold,
There, I know, the hopeful arch,
In its stately cross-sky march,
  Deep has trod its seeds of gold.

MY SUNFLOWER

Out upon the sunburnt plains,
Fringing all the roads and lanes,
Whisp'ring nights to lonesome swains
On their creaking, groaning wains,
Catching at their horses' manes,
  Like coy fairies,
Grows a simple, comely flower,
Child of heaven's golden dower,
Born in some delightsome hour
When a transient summer shower
Changed as if by magic power
  All the prairies.

Sunlit halo round its face,
Strong, of hardy, frontier race,
Straight, but of becoming grace,
Tall, as when the gilded mace
Rises o'er the populace
  Agitated;
Parsee priest and clock in one,
Following the regnant sun
From the morn till day is done,
As devout as patt'ring nun
Seeking daily benison,
  Never sated.

Worshiper of heaven's light,
Art thou Zoroaster's sprite,
Seeking in thy constant flight
Lands where never comes the night,
Where thy face shall ne'er lose sight
        Of the Sun God?
Ah! my child, I see thee there,
Golden-haloed, wondrous fair,
Looking always from life's care
Toward the light that burns fore'er
In the realm to which thou'rt heir
        Of the one God!

A BIRTHDAY PRAYER

Keep this little light, oh Father,
  Burning year on year—
Driving back the dark about it
  With its rays of cheer.

Keep these little feet, oh Father,
  Standing here to-day
By the side of life's first mile-stone,
  Always in Thy way.

Keep this little heart, oh Father,
  Loving, pure, and true,
That when come the evening shadows
  Naught shall be to rue.

Keep this little one, oh Father,
  Near me through life's task—
In His name, who blessed the children,
  This I humbly ask.

TO HER MOTHER

How deep's the sea?
How deep?   Ah me,
　For plummet!—
As deep as sky
Or cloud is high,
　Or summit
Of yon tall peak
That aye doth seek
　Its double
Beneath the sea
When it is free
　From trouble.

How deep's the sea
Love's argosy
　Doth travel?
No pen of mine
Can rhythmic line
　Unravel,
That's long enough
Or strong enough
　To measure—
As deep, my love,
As thou'rt above
　All treasure.

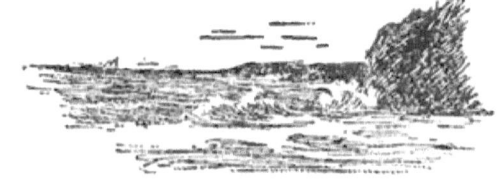

FROM
GOD'S MEADOW

A load of new-mown clover hay
    Passed down a city street,
Where men are busy all the day
    In buying, selling wheat—
The wheat that grows but in the brains
    Of those who sell or buy,
That never catches heaven's rains
    Nor hears the reaper's sigh,—
Where multitudes in frenzy rage
    Beneath the oriflamme
Of Fortune blind who throws the gage
    To prosper or to damn;
Here passed the fragrant meadow load,
    All redolent of June,
Just when the offices o'erflowed
    Upon the street at noon;
And many a rushing broker stopped
    To catch the sweetened breeze,
 As if o'er heaven's walls had dropped
    Some blossoms from its trees.—
The wheat, the gold are quite forgot,
    The clover's round his feet,
 The light of boyhood days is shot
    Adown that darkened street.

So when along my narrow way
    Of homely drudgery,
Hemmed in by walls that dark the day
    Of what my life would be,
There come the toddling steps of one
    From far celestial mead,
Whose face like burnished morning sun,
    From drowsy vigils freed,
Through all the gloomy corners trails
    The light of that fair land—
Who brings the breath of scented vales
    By whispering forests fanned;
Then Earth, which was but darkened street
    Of sordid entities,
Becomes a trysting place where meet
    The two Eternities.

AT EIGHTEEN
MONTHS

My Ellen's eighteen months to-day;
Good Father Time, canst thou not stay
The gently dropping grains of sand
And pass with thy transforming hand
This image of the woman grown,
This little queen upon her throne,
Who tries in primal speech to tell
Her wants, her joys—her woes as well—
Who toddles, tumbles when she walks,
Whose laugh the rippling brooklet mocks,
Who puts her lips close to my ear
And tells me what none else may hear
About the fairies that she sees
About the dogs and birds and trees?
Oh stay thy hand, Good Father, stay,
And leave her as she is to-day,
A baby-girl of eighteen moons,
The best of all God's blessed boons—
    My baby Ellen.

AT EIGHTEEN
YEARS

My Ellen's eighteen years to-night,
For Time in dreams has dimmed my sight;
He does not listen to my prayer,
He turns his glass for answer—there!
My Ellen stands a maiden now—
Her mother's eyes, her mother's brow.
She thrills a multitude with song,
Or with her fingers holds the throng;
There's music even when she talks,
There's grace and beauty when she walks.
She's fair; her features wear no mask;
She's all that parent's heart could ask.
Again her lips approach my ear—
There are no other words more dear—
No! do not stay thy hand for me,
But make her what my dreams foresee,
A happy maid of eighteen years,
In whom all loveliness appears—
　　　My daughter Ellen.

THE STREET WHERE I DWELL

The street where I dwell is long,
The street where I dwell is wide;
From sky to sky
It travels by
Great trees of green
That forward lean
To fleck with shade
This way, man-made,
Where once grew rank,
By brooklet's bank,
The prairie grass;
Where Indian lass
Plucked flowers, wild grown,
By Heaven sown,
And tawny brave
His arrow drave
At bird or beast
For savage feast;—
I like no way in all the world beside
As this my street,
Where little feet
Run down to meet
My homeward steps at eventide.

The street where I dwell is long,
The street where I dwell is wide;
The blue skies bend
To tell my end
And whence I came,
For fleet or lame

But journey I
From sky to sky,
As journeyed they
Who trod this way
In other days,
And, hid by haze
That dims our sight,
Roam fields bedight
With brighter flowers,
Or hunt for hours
The caribou
Of Manitou;—
I'd love not Heaven with all its joy, beside,
Though gold its street,
If little feet
Came not to meet
My homeward steps at eventide.

THE FIRE-WORSHIPER

Dear is the fire that burns afar
In blazing sun, in silent star;
    But a dearer fire
    Is the dreamy pyre
That burns on my own hearthstone.

Dear is the ray of beacon light
That warns the mariner by night;
    But a dearer ray
    Is that lights the way
To rest at my own threshold.

Dear is the flame of candles tall
O'er banquet board in festal hall;
    But a dearer flame
    I, a bookman, claim—
That burns at my own bed's head.

Dear is the light of amethyst,
Or paler gem that tells of tryst;
    But a dearer light
    Is that flashes bright
Beneath my Ellen's eyelids.

LINES TO MY BICYCLE

My chiefest pride
Is father's "Ide"
—"Our Special Ide"—
Which we bestride,
Beatified,
And tandem glide,
Quite satisfied
To ride and ride
A "Special Ide"
    Forever.

As high and low
We gaily go,
The breezes blow,
The cattle low,
The babies crow,
The farmers "whoa,"
Electrified
To see us ride
A "Special Ide"
    Together.

Hack, wagon, dray,
Give right of way,
None say me nay;
I hold full sway,
Brook no delay;
All quick obey,
Quite terrified
Whene'er I ride
The "Special Ide"
    With father.

This is for me
The greatest glee,
To spin with thee,
At father's knee,
Past flower and tree
Past bird and bee,
O "Special Ide"
My joy and pride,—
There is beside
    None other!

And when the night
Turns out the light,
And pillows white
To sleep invite,
In cycling flight
I still delight,
Unsatisfied;
And still I ride
A "Special Ide"
    In Dreamland.

TO "LITTLE GIRLIE"

I walked one spring-time morning all alone
  To where the flowers their heads in winter hide,
But gloomily, though sky with sunlight shone,
  For Little Girlie was not at my side.

The Robin hopped about, sedate and sad—
  He'd waited vainly for her voice since dawn;
The Meadow-lark in notes no longer glad
  Sang "Where, oh where, has Little Girlie gone?"

The Pansies turned their faces anxiously,
  The Roses whispered as I passed their way,
The Daffodils and Lilies asked of me,
  "Oh where is sweet-voiced Little Girlie, pray?"

Then came the Flowers that she loved best, I knew,
  With eyes as blue as Little Girlie's own,
And they were filled with tears of morning dew,
  For they had spied that I was there alone.

I spoke, and quick their faces all grew bright:
  "Our Little Girlie's gone to country far,
"But you, sweet Flowers, shall go to her dear sight
  "To bear our love and tell how lone we are."

WHEN THERE WERE THREE CANDLES

—

A
LITTLE DINNER
given by
A LITTLE LADY
on
HER THIRD BIRTHDAY
to
HER LITTLE FRIENDS
of the School
for
LITTLE FOLKS
March 10
1897

—

MENU:

There was a good woman (you know her name, too),
She had so many children she didn't know what to do;
So she gave them some
BROTH
And . . . with . . . it . . . some
BREAD
and
COOKIES
And . . . ORANGES . . . sweet,
Then . . . instead
of a . . . . WHIPPING . . all 'round
She . . . gave . . . a . . . sweet
KISS
To every small boy and every wee miss.
I think she's far better, and I'm sure you do, too,
Than the cruel old woman that lived in the shoe.

The Stranger

THE STRANGER

A stranger came she to our door
   And straight we took her in,
A traveler from a foreign shore,
   With neither kith nor kin.

Scant clothed was she for this cold earth,
   Scant thatched her little head,
But soon in ermine was she girth
   And laid in eider bed.

We gave her drink and food fore-stored
   To feed such travelers;
We kissed the stranger and implored
   Our blessings might be hers.

Who aught hath done to these, the least,
   "Hath done it unto Me",—
Whoso hath clothed or given feast
   Or healed or set men free.

And is our Heaven completely won
   By such sweet ministries?
Perchance 'tis so our Heaven's begun
   'Mid earth's perplexities.

MARGET : A HARVEST LULLABY

Sleep ye, my Marget,
  Sleep ye, my sweet;
Hearken! the cricket
  Sings in the wheat!

> *Cheep, cricket, cheep,*
>   *Cradle your wheat;*
> *Sleep, Marget, sleep,*
>   *My Marguerite.*

Sleep ye, my Marget,
  Sleep ye, my love;
Deep grow the shadows,
  Stars peep above.

> *Creep, shadows, creep,*
>   *Over the skies;*
> *Sleep, Marget, sleep,*
>   *Shut your blue eyes.*

Sleep ye, my Marget,
  Hush ye, your cry;
See Father's sickle
  Hangs in the sky.

> *Reap, sickle, reap*
>   *Blessings for thee;*
> *Sleep, Marget, sleep,*
>   *My Margery.*

Sleep ye, my Marget,
  Sleep ye, my pearl,
Sleep ye my precious
  Darling wee girl.

> *Keep, angels, keep*
>   *Watch o'er my pet;*
> *Sleep, Marget, sleep,*
>   *My Margaret.*

Not long it is since she went forth
  From Heaven's fairest firth,
And sailed on clouds by west and north
  For fairest spot of Earth.

Not long—but she has found it fair,
  And full of loving friends,
And to these all she bids me bear
  The love her kind heart sends.

But I am very slow of pen—
  To all I can't indite
The measure of her love—but then,
  Your love she does requite.

Marian and Ellen

A NEIGHBORHOOD SHOWER

Fair is the day,
  Skies azure hue,
Happy at play
  Black eyes and blue.

Dark grows the day,
  Skies lower, alack!
Ended their play,
  Blue eyes and black.

Swift follows rain,
  Homeward these two—
At window pane
  Black eyes and blue.

Soon the shower's o'er,
  Sunshine comes back,
Tears fill no more
  Blue eyes and black.

Whose are the black?
  Marian's,—bright
As meteor's track
  On winter's night.

Whose are the blue?
  Ellen's,—deep
As heaven's hue
  In summer sleep.

Rebecca

TO REBECCA

"Becky," she's a rare, good child,
  Daughter of the prairie,
Sweet as flowers that there grow wild,
  Happy as a fairy.

Summers lives she far away,
  Where the fields are sunny;
Just where fairies like to stay—
  Where the bees find honey.

Winters lives she snug at home,
  Just where fairies would be,
When the bees are in the comb—
  If they always could be!

So my "Becky" flits about
  'Tween the farm and city,
Sipping sweets to give them out—
  "Becky," bright and pretty.

When you see my "Becky" clad
  In her garments airy,
You will think a glimpse you've had
  Of a real live fairy.

Dorothy

TO DOROTHY

Oh, Dorothy, Dorothy, Double-U,
I'm very reluctant to trouble you,—
But there is one thing I should like to know
And perhaps you can tell me whether 'tis so.

Are you a daughter of Eight-six,
The class of your father—very prolix
In virtues and talents and strong of mind,—
Genius and virtue in one combined?

Oh, Dorothy, brown-eyed, red-cheeked lass,
Are you a daughter of this great class—
The greatest and brightest since Eighty-two,
(Or so they think and of course you do)?

Or are you a daughter of Eighty-seven,
Your mother's class, that like unto leaven
Is spreading all over this lump of earth
To make it a place of larger worth?

A class that commingles with charity
Rare beauty, and keeps them at parity;
That isn't contented with what's within reach,
But Brahmin and Turk is trying to teach.

Or are you a daughter of both, forsooth?
—Ah, there I think I have hit the truth,
That beauty and charity rare you mix
With the mental strength of Eighty-six.

Oh, Dorothy, Dorothy, Double-U,
You're fortunate very if this is true,
And may you transmit to Nineteen-eleven
The best of both Eighty-six and -seven.

Ruth

TO RUTH

Ruth, dear, winsome little Ruth,
Would you like to know the truth?
Then I'll tell it you, forsooth,
        Little Ruth:
I love very little girls
That have pretty golden curls
More than boys; for girls are pearls,
        Little Ruth,
Tossed up from God's ocean deep,
Left 'mid sand by tide at neap
On the shore, for us to keep,
        Little Ruth,
Till God wants them back, forsooth,—
This is what I think's the truth,
Ruth, my precious little Ruth,
        Little Ruth.

My Cousin William (and Preston)

MY COUSIN WILLIAM

My Cousin William is my Uncle William's son,
So is the story of his precious life begun—
    Unless you're fond of archaeology
And wish to trace his lineage still farther back,
In which event you'll find you're on King Wil-
    liam's track,
    King Will of Norman genealogy.

My Cousin William's sober as a county judge
And all my girlish pranks he but pronounces
    "fudge,"—
    As solemn as the church doxology.
Some day, perhaps, he'll sit upon the supreme
    bench,
Or else with cold and stately arguments he'll
    quench
    All those who're wrong in their theology.

At any rate, my Cousin William will be great;
Some day, who knows, he may be Gov'nor of the
    State;
    Perchance, Professor of Psychology
In some great college, such as Knox; or own a bank,
Or be a wholesale merchant of the foremost rank,
    Or write a book on ichthyology.

My Cousin William is the coming man, no doubt,
And I'm the coming woman who is talked about
    And talked about, with much tautology;
But if my cousin is as good as his pa-pa,
And I'm as sweet and kind as my mam-ma,—
    We'll not be 'shamed of our necrology.

Louise

TO LOUISE*

These quaint and dainty little girls,
In kerchief, cap and peeping curls,
   Just come from o'er the seas,
I send with these sweet flowers to tell
The love I cannot speak so well,—
   My love for dear Louise.

Though falling snows drift deep about,
Though winds blow cold and chill without,
   And stark stand all the trees,
Still like the amaranth of old
These flowers shall bloom through heat and cold—
   Shall bloom for sweet Louise.

The snows have drifted deep about,
The winds blown cold and chill without,
   And stark stand all the trees;
But at His upper mansion's gate,
These messengers shall daily wait
   With flowers for our Louise.

---

*Sent with Grust's picture of two girls carrying hyacinths and pinks, to Louise.

TO ALBERT

You've heard of Albert, Prince of Wales,
  Victoria's petted son,
Who cares not that the kingdom fails
  If but his horse has won;

Who's getting rather bald and stout,
  And sometimes fears lest he
May after all not quite live out
  Another jubilee;

Who's fond of dinners, fond of clothes,
  This grown-up child of Guelph,
Who's fond of golf, who labor loathes,
  Who's fondest of himself.

He's not the Albert that I mean;
  Mine is a Prince of Boys, not Wales,
And he's the son, too, of a queen
  Whose jar of cookies never fails.

A first-rate head's beneath his crown
  Whene'er his ample hat is on;
He's quite the best boy in our town,
  And I'm—well I'm his "Uncle John."

THE FAMOUS RIDE OF CORPORAL PARK AND LITTLE PHIL

Up from their beds at break of day
There leaped two boys and straightaway
They groomed their horses, "Field" and "Ide,"
For they had vowed 'fore night to ride
    To Sheffield, four and fifty miles away.

They mounted each his iron steed,
All cleaned and oiled for lightning speed,—
Then up they spun Wataga's road
While horses shied and farmers "whoaed"—
    And Sheffield five and forty miles away.

Despatches sent to mothers dear,
Again they mount and soon they near
Oneida's stores, where they must stop
To lunch on cakes and ice cold pop—
    With Sheffield only forty miles away.

Down dale, up hill they gaily go,
On "Ide" and "Field," now fast, now slow,
And soon they run a-spinning down
The streets of staid Altona town,—
   And Sheffield five and thirty miles away.

With pumping tired, with hunger gaunt,
They reach a Galva restaurant,
Sandwich and steak and milk and pie
Soon disappear, with many a sigh
   For Sheffield, five and twenty miles away.

Again they start with rested heels,
No one is tired (except their wheels),
But wheels go faster when they're tired,
And boys when properly inspired;
   Yet Sheffield's more than fifteen miles away.

The road is rough, the way is steep—
Legs, arms and wheels all in a heap—
But heroes are not daunted so,
They're up again and on they go
   To Sheffield, now but seven miles away.

At length they climb the last steep hill,
Brave Corp'ral Park and Little Phil;
Sheffield is theirs; the battle's won;
And now for two days' solid fun
   With Galesburg four and fifty miles away.

TO EU-NI-CE

Every shrub and prairie tree,
Whether flower or berry be
   The gift you bear;
Don your best for Eu-ni-ce,—
   Blossoms in your hair.

Hum your hymn, oh honey bee,
Dandelions, money free
   Coin ye on the green,
For the dainty Eu-ni-ce,
   For the little queen.

Children dance in jollity,
Join in glad equality,
   This joyous day;
Dance around fair Eu-ni-ce,
   The queen of May.

TO FLORIBEL: MY PILOT

Here I sit as sole dictator
  Of the little world I know,
Wand'ring as a navigator
  Whither gentle winds may blow,
        With my Floribel.

Floribel is Palinurus,
  Good as gold and true as steel,
And no rocks will ever lure us
  While she's standing at the wheel,
        My good Floribel.

Thus, in fair or cloudy weather
  Daily we perambulate,
(*Per* and *ambulo*) together,
  Galesburg streets in regal state—
        I with Floribel.

Do you wonder at my Latin?
  Straight it came from Miss McCall,
For I've learned it as I've sat in
  This same place—I've learned it all
        From my Floribel.

All the world's a panorama
  'Fore my wicker-wheeled throne,
And the children act a drama
  Daily for me and my own,
        My dear Floribel.

Some day, dear perambulator,
  Many things will part us two,
And some other navigator,
  He will sail away with you
        And my Floribel.

TO THE MAN OF THE HOUSE
WITH THE SKYWARD WINDOW

"And thou shalt call him John
  "And joy thou'lt have and gladness,"
So spoke an angel long agone
  To priest who lived in sadness,
Because no son had come to him
  To minister at altar,
To take his place when eye grew dim
  And voice began to falter.

And thou, oh priest of this new day,
  Who in His temple dwellest,
Who first dost hear what God doth say
  And then to mankind tellest—
As thou hast called thine offspring "John,"
  So may he banish sadness,
May he be herald of the dawn
  Of thy great day of gladness.

And when thine eyes age-dimmed shall be,
  And cannot see the star-light,
When with an inner eye thou'lt see
  The gleaming of a far light;
May he, whom thou hast given this name,
  Stand in thy lab'ratory,
Which temple is, and thence proclaim
  The coming of His glory.

THE ANGELS, THE STAR, AND THE VISION

THE ANGELS

The angels of God came to earth one night,
  But they found all the world asleep,
Until they approached in their shining flight
  Where the shepherds were watching their sheep.

The fisherman dreamt of the morrow's draught,
  And the trader, he dreamt of gold;
The ploughman aloud in his slumber laughed
  As he thought of the "hundred fold."

The angels of God all of these passed by,
  A-dreaming of fishes and crops;
They sang of the Christ from that midnight sky
  To the men on the lone hill tops.

THE STAR

A star ventured forth on a strange, new way,
  From a far-away firmament,
And hastened to find where the young child lay,
  As it swept from the Orient.

The fisherman dreamt of his shining draught,
  And the trader of coffers filled;
The ploughman again in his slumber laughed
  As he dreamt of the barns he'd build.

The Orient star gave no light for them,
  For their troubles had closed their eyes;
The star drew alone to Bethlehem
  The men who were watching the skies.

THE VISION

The shepherds beheld with their heads all bared,
  And the wise men worshiped afar;
The shepherds their flocks left alone, uncared,
  And the wise men followed His star.

The fisherman goes to his daily toil,
  While the merchant for trade prepares;
The ploughman returns to his stony soil—
  The Christ had come unawares.

So, child, it is in the land of men:
  They are blest who oft look above;
'Tis when we look up, and 'tis only then,
  We have visions of God's great love.

If o'er a precipice thou find'st thy way,
Look up; a downward glance will bring dismay
    And certain death;
        Courage, child, courage!

Or if across a plain thy way doth lead,
Look out, not in; beholding other's need
    Forget thine own;
        Courage, child, courage!

But whether precipice or plain thy path,
Look forward with brave heart; he victory hath
    Who ne'er looks back;
        Courage, child, courage!

FINLEY